The

Night Hound

A.C. Winfield

The Night Hound

ISBN-13: 978-1530229291
ISBN-10: 1530229294

For Enya x

Acknowledgements

To all my family and friends. Without your support and encouraging words I would not have been able to create such characters, nor, had courage to tell their stories.
To Ben, for all your love and support throughout the past few months. This winter have been one hard slog to get so many books ready but we accomplished it together. Thank you!
Thank you to my readers who continue to enjoy my books. I hope I will never disappoint you.
Ax.

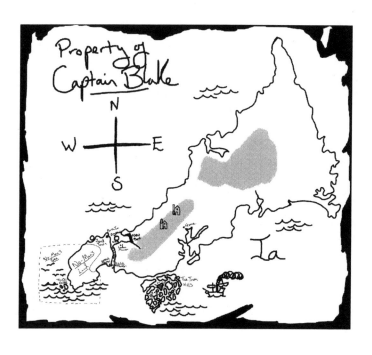

The Night Hound

*O*n Ia's seas, two mighty ships met. Their chimneys billowed thick, dark smoke in an angry fashion. Fluttering in the wind were two makeshift white flags. Instead of signalling peace however, the two flags unnaturally met, flapping at one another, sending tiny threads flying off in all directions as they tore each other apart. A forced treaty that not even the steam ships seemed to be able to uphold.

1

As three members of the Fire Crows' crew entered the quarters of Amber Jade, captain of the White Gull, one snarled her sharp white teeth, another narrowed his deep sea blue eyes and the other was so tall, he had to duck underneath the wooden beams to walk in.

Captain Blake was the first to speak. "Amber Jade." Pain and despair echoed in those words, so much so that they betrayed the captain's true feelings which he desperately tried to hide deep down inside. Amber Jade's jade-green eyes flashed as she looked up from where she sat behind her sun-kissed chestnut desk.

"Ah, brother, glad you could make it." She smiled. Her tone seemed friendly enough but all three knew the malice she held deep within, caged like a wild animal.

"I am not your brother." Blake corrected her quietly, his eyes flashing a warning.

"Not through blood, no." She answered darkly. Her long nails gripping into the hard desk for a few moments and then, her shoulders seemed to relax as she took in the others before her. Many wouldn't find it relaxing with a giant of a man and a giant form of a Star Bear in their cabin but not this Lady Captain.

"AJ, why have you done this?" The giant man's voice was slightly muffled through his thick, bushy beard. His eyes glistened as a thick, pearly tear rolled down the side of his cheek. He quickly wiped it away, hoping no one saw. But it was too late, they already had.

"Because, Father," She said the word with such repulsiveness Bob Macy's heart gave a huge painful throb. "This was the only way of getting you all to do as you are told." A deep growl reverberated across the room, rattling the doors, walls and even the large porthole windows framed in thick brass. No one needed to check where it was coming from. "Brother, kindly keep your pet under control or else I will call this meeting to an end in a way neither you nor the Bear will enjoy." Neither word was spoken to quieten Stella Maris, the Northern Star in a Star Bear form but just the thought of the possible consequences made her voice die away. In a flurry of bright, white snowflakes, the Star Bear transformed into a beautiful lady wearing a midnight-blue dress, studded with sequins shining as brightly as the stars outside the hot room. "Better." AJ smiled a smile that went up on one side. It was Stella's heart who now gave a painful throb this time, for she recognised that smile.

Deep inside Stella, the Star Bear clawed at the corners of her mind, fighting to get out to attack the terrible woman but she was far too used to controlling her Star Bear's desires… even if they did reflect her own true feelings.

"If you have touched a single hair on her head…" The threat held in the air for Stella was cut off by

Captain Blake, her husband as he took hold of her tiny wrist in his salt-encrusted hand. Stella's head swivelled sharply in the captain's direction but he didn't look at her, he was watching the female captain very closely.

"You said if we met...you reassured us Ebony would be safe. How do we know you haven't just let the fire take her?" Stella couldn't say any more. Her eyes glistening, now fixed on to Amber Jade as they waited with bated breath for her reply. The horrifying memory of the fire's damage danced across Stella's mind.

The Lady Captain nodded in the direction of an open door at the back of her cabin, signalling someone to bring something, or in this case, someone into the lamp light. The three turned in unison, their hearts filling momentarily with false hope. A small cage was presented to them. The member of Amber Jade's crew, a young lad, placed the cage on the sun-kissed desk. His captain's jade-green eyes brightened as she inclined her amber-coloured head of hair towards the creature held within. Even Stella's light seemed to dim, her startling white snowflakes fizzling into thin air as she saw how poorly one of her own kind was being treated. If the crew of Amber Jade did this to him, then how were they treating her own daughter? The trail of thoughts evaporated away as Captain Amber Jade reached into the small cage and was greeted by an almighty MEOW! Stella felt her bear hum with pleasure as the cruel woman winced in pain as the small creature's claws struck her once, twice, three times but still she did not let go as she jerked out the twin-tailed Comet Cat, Hale, by the scruff of his tiny neck roughly. They could see in the candlelight how matted his once glossy fur coat was. The Star Bear within Stella roared so loudly Stella couldn't help but to wince. "Now sweet little Comet Cat," began the Lady Captain, their green eyes meeting one another. "Tell them how safe Ebony, my dear little niece is." The Lady Captain smiled falsely sweet as she placed the poor, ragged form of the Comet Cat on the table, stroking his back with clawed hands, making it impossible for him to escape. All four of them grew numb.

"Tell them how well I am looking after you both." Captain Amber Jade now turned her jade-green eyes towards the three standing in front of her desk. Captain Blake of the pirate steam ship Fire Crow, her step-brother. Stella, a Star Bear in human form, her sister-in-law and her own father, Bob Macy. In an impossible reality this would have been a great reunion after all these long years of separation but now they were enemies. Watching them closely to make sure they had received the message loud and clear, Amber Jade was enjoying every second as the three found their world falling apart, piece by heart shattering piece.

The little Comet Cat, far too scared, stayed silent.

"Tell them!" She picked up the little black cat up by the scruff of his neck roughly. Amber Jade's face was thunderous, a bubbling sea underneath a blackened, stormy sky. "Fine." She said. With one swift movement she shoved the little black cat back into the tiny, cramped cage once again. Flinging the cage into her crew member's arms she half-bellowed. "If you won't cooperate…" She paused, thinking for a moment before smiling sickly in the candle light. "Make sure he's put away so he never sees the stars' light again." The little Comet Cat began to yowl loudly, finding his voice once again as he tried to fight his way out. Even over all the noise, Stella's sobs could still be heard. Her heart torn in two for the little Comet Cat. She knew of the torture it would be for a star creature like herself to never see the night sky again but she was powerless, unable to act against Amber Jade if she was to assure her daughter's safe return. The cat's emerald-green eyes met her soft golden flecked brown. A silent forgiveness passed between the two of them.

The young lad bowed his head to his mistress and hurried out the door. There was a sudden movement from her male guests, but Amber Jade had them just how she liked them. Scared. All this captain had to do to stop them from attacking her was to raise one finger, "Now, now." She said playfully, wiggling her finger from side to side, tutting at them like naughty school children. "If you attack me now however do you think you will you get to see poor, sweet Ebony ever again? You know, my Masters can destroy her just like…" She clicked her fingers. The sound pieced all three of their hearts. Even Stella's Star Bear deep inside doubled over in pain, making Stella grip momentarily onto her husband's arm for support. Amber Jade laughed, a cruel cackle that neither her step-brother nor her own father, recognised from the once sweet girl they both used to know.

"So, after all these years, after everything, you are now working for the Council of Ia!" Blake roared at Amber Jade as she made her way over to a little hatch, a heating vent which Blake knew ran all the way down to the boiler room. He knew all the ins and outs as he had built this ship, many years ago. To see it now under such a cruel mistress was distressing for Captain Blake of the Fire Crow, for he believed all ships had a heart and soul, just like you and I.

Amber Jade stopped, looked at Blake in surprise and then doubled over in high pitched laughter once again. The three looked at one another confused.

"The Council of Ia? Oh brother, you do make me laugh." She said, wiping a happy tear away. "The members of Ia's Council may have chosen to work with you once in the time of the Great War all those years ago. Trying to defeat the Eternals. Losing many men, woman and loved ones' blah, blah, blah." Blake grew mad, his hands shaking as Amber Jade waved her own in the air as if hundreds of souls lost forever wasn't a concern of hers. "But you forget, the Council hate pirates. There may be a truce between you and those who follow you. A rule generally summed up as 'you stay out of my hair and I stay out of yours'," she said, flicking her short amber-coloured hair. "But you, your pet...," Stella growled, despite being in human form. Amber Jade tutted. "That temper will lead you into trouble. Where was I? Oh yes!" Her teeth seemed to glow eerily with delight from the lantern hanging above her. "But all of you who were in this little secret of yours knows if the Council ever found out who Ebony really was, heard her prophecy maybe, your treaty will collapse. That tincey, wincey bit of evidence is all they needed to be persuaded."

"You betrayed your own family!" Bob Macy bellowed making the whole room shake. A map of Ia in a frame rocked back and forth till it hung crooked. He spat at his own daughter's feet. The droplets of saliva sizzled on the metal of the hatch.

"Gross, really Father? What kind of hello is that after all these years? But yes, in a way. You forget, Father, of our upbringing. The old ways of the piracy." Even in the flickering light the Lady Captain could see the giant man's face burn, his whole body shaking.

"That's... that's in the past. Things have changed. For the better, Blake has shown us that."

"Yes, things have certainly changed. Haven't they, old man?"

Amber Jade continued laughing at her cruel joke as she kicked open the small, round heating vent. "Here you'll find all the answers you are look for..."

11

She signalled for them all to look. Hesitantly the pirate, Captain Blake of the pirate steam ship Fire Crow, Stella Maris, a Star Bear in human form and the giant pirate, Bob Macy slowly made their way forwards, knowing that somehow this was a clue to Ebony's whereabouts.

Blake's eyes were transfixed. It felt as if his whole life gravitated to this one moment in time. All three of their hearts pounded loudly until the sound filled the wooden cladded room with one rhythmic beat. Captain Blake felt the seas current swirl outside the wooden hull below, the white crested waves momentary freezing in their course, reflecting his nerves.

As the captain and his wife, Stella Maris cast their eyes down the narrow, deep, dark shaft, so dark it took a little while for even their keen eyes to adjust, a shadow moved way down below. A moment later, dimly at first something was glowing but as it grew brighter and brighter, they saw it flicker, no, blink up at them… it was an eye!

The eye focused on their faces, scanning them as though for an impossible moment, the creature recognised them deep within. Blake's heart squeezed as hard as Stella's grip on his arm but he did not take any notice of the pain either one of them had caused. He understood what Amber Jade had done. He would recognise those warm brown, golden flecked eyes anywhere. Even with the reddish glow.

Suddenly the golden flecked eyes vanished, a swish of movement picked up by both the husband's and wife's unhuman sharp ears. A mighty roar rose from the chamber deep down below. The ship shook. Shearing heat as flames raced up towards them. Rolling and clawing their way up the narrow circular wall of the vent. Blake didn't move. Everything was clicking into place. Now knowing what Amber Jade, his once friend who he considered as a sister all those long lost years ago, had done. His world fell apart.

Amber Jade kicked the vent closed just before the flames could grapple their way over the top. With a loud clang she gained their attention once again. The look on their faces brought a shrill of unrecognisable laughter to her rosy, red lips. An uncomfortable heat rose from the vent as it glowed the same luminous red as the creature's eyes.

13

"Beautiful, isn't she?" Amber Jade asked, licking her lips, savouring the tension in the air. Beads of sweat pearled on all of their brows. Blake lifted his head. His deep, sea-blue eyes transfixed on her jade-green as they glowed unnaturally in the magenta light. Before Blake had time to think, he had unsheathed his concealed sword and slammed his step-sister against the wall, making the tilted picture fall with an almighty crash. The sword's sharp tip glittered threateningly as it rested just below her chin. Amber Jade however, showed no fear but giggled as though the sword was merely a feather tickling her. Crimson beaded where her skin rubbed against the sharpened edge.

"Traitor!" Blake bellowed in her face. What she said next made Stella's Star Bear reform in a flurry of falling snow and Bob Macy to shake even more.

"Oh brother, you might have finally got it but clearly these two idiots certainly don't." She tried to push her step-brother's sword away but Blake was far too strong, even for this sea captain. Amber Jade frowned, her lips pursing in a mocked sulk up at her once-brother. "Fine, I offered the Council my help."

She started to explain, clearly enjoying every moment of their misery. Blake was so close to the female captain's face now he could see the lines etched across her skin, showing her true age. How old was she when he boarded Bob Macy's ship? For a moment the captain's mind was lost to the past... "I showed them what they needed to see." She said, bringing him back down with a tremendous bump. "The truth about the secrets the old man was hiding. Rufus Night might have told them Ebony was a daughter of his long lost son, James Night but the truth was she was the daughter of those touched by the gods. Fathered by a pirate who should have died when he was cast into the sea as a baby." Blake slammed Amber Jade into the wooden wall once again, trying to shut her up. It was too painful for him to hear about his past coming from her poisonous lips. Amber Jade's grin widened despite the knock on the head. "Whom he was mothered by the..." Blake had enough, he wedged his sword's edge in deeper.

"I swear I will kill you if you don't stop piping on." He told her through gritted teeth. The captain had never felt as angry in all his long life as he watched his sister's jade-green eyes shine with malice.

A giant hand squeezed his shoulder. "Son," Blake took an unsteady breath. It had been such a long time since he heard that word. "We need to hear what she has to say. For Ebony's sake."

16

The seconds ticked by, Blake could feel all their eyes on him now. Slowly his sword lost its sting on Amber Jade's throat.

"Glad you listened to reason." She said, wiping at the cut.

"Tell us what you did AJ, or I might allow Blake to shut you up forever."

"Oh Father, you were always overdramatic." She said cheerfully, hugging the giant of a man in such a way he forgot why they were there. For a moment the old giant pirate thought he had his daughter back but Blake knew Amber Jade's games. Catching hold of her shoulder, he threw AJ away before the pirate could wrap his own arms around her lovingly.

"Tell us what you did!"

"Very well." She said with such coolness. Despite the heat coming from the furnace below, the temperature dropped, making all their hairs stand up on end. "As I was saying." AJ sat back into her captain's chair, her booted feet banging hard against her deck's surface as she made herself at home. "A pregnant woman," She waved her hand at the Star Bear Stella. "Carrying the soul of the lost star Ursa

17

Minor himself, giving the baby, Ebony, powers no one, not even the stars themselves could foresee. Legendary powers that is. If you believe the tales that is, to hold the balance between the stars, Ia and the Underverse itself... Ebony's Legacy, if you like. I quite like that title, don't you?" She winked up at Blake. Amber Jade's eyes scanned the three standing in front of her. Not one of them looked impressed with her naming the girl's prophecy. "No? Oh it's so hard to please some people these days. Very well." She said, waving her hand again before placing them behind her head. "Maybe you'll like the next bit of my story." The three watched on with bated breath as Amber Jade reclined even further, getting comfortable in her chair as she continued telling them her story. "At first the Council laughed, of course. What a most unbelievable story to come from such a person but when they saw the truth," she winked at Stella who growled loudly in return. "In return for this. Well, let's just say the Council turned a blind eye. Come on," The fire-haired captain said, swinging her legs off the table and leaning forwards in a dramatic fashion as though she was telling them a scary bedtime story "Do you not see? You do, don't you brother?" She asked, licking her rosy lips. She could see the turbulent sea reflected in his deep blue eyes and it made her happy! "Yes, I did want to see that idiotic Rufus Night to fall but I do not work for the Council." Her focus now on Stella as she watched the woman inside the nightly Star Bear's eyes cry out her daughter's name inside. "My Masters are much more powerful than any of you. The Eternals are rising and with my tiniest bit of help, their Carrion army are coming." Amber Jade leaned back in her comfy chair. Placing her feet back up on the table, denting its sun-kissed surface with her heavy boots as she watched the three realise not only did she, Captain Amber Jade, hold the girl's fate in her salt encrusted hands but the whole of Ia's as well and she couldn't have been happier.

***

Meanwhile, far below the depths of the sea, below the many layers of rock formation and deeper than the deepest mine, you'll find the end of the seemingly impassable Labyrinth. There lies a seemingly impossible land, the Underverse.

Not much is understood about the labyrinth or the Underverse, even to those that occupy the land but many would probably think of a hellish pit filled with darkness, pain and misery but the contrary was true.

The days and nights roll into one, as, in the Underverse there are no stars, moon, not even a sun. Just darkness way up high and down to the black sea that surround the spectacular kingdom. It was the land itself that produced the Underverse's light in a wide spectrum of colour. Every little thing much brighter and bolder no human eye has ever seen up on the surface.

Each leaf, blade of grass and trickling stream glowing brightly during the day and then dully during the night. This was the only distinction between the Underverse's day and night.

The land was seemingly empty apart from a pack of magnificent creatures that roamed the Underverse. The Night Hounds...

***

A Night Hound howled.

One after the other they howled together, reconnecting their bond, their pack.

PACK, PACK, PACK the call pulled at the Night Hounds internally, instinctively.

The largest of them all, his fur coat showing his age despite his eternal life, threw back his head and howled. The call from the pack was so enticing, so intense he could no longer resist the urge to howl at the pitch-black sky high above.

Finally, he and his pack stopped in their wild call. The Night Hound was alone, on the edge of a cliff. Water rushed past his feet, hurling itself over the edge and into the black sea way down below. The black liquid reflecting the land's shimmering array of colours like slick oil tumbled over the edge. The waterfall was wide and filled with the black water's vapours. Again reflecting the vast spectrum of colours in the shimmering landscape around him.

Looking around, the largest of the Night Hounds could see for miles. The jagged, pointed cliffs. Trees gripping on tightly by their roots deep into the rusty red earth. To us, it would have been a spectacular sight to see but the old Night Hound didn't care for the spectacular view. The Night Hounds didn't feel a thing. They could not feel the cold nor any emotion. All the pack's Alpha knew was the importance of his pack. He had been here far too long... Or so he thought.

Another howl. Then another, then another.

He found his ears twitching, lips snarling. A deep rumble in his chest, vibrating his entire body. For all this Night Hound's existence nothing had changed until now. Something was wrong...

Alpha! Alpha! Alpha! They called to him.

The leader of all the Night Hounds flashed his fangs, licked his thick, black lips and started running so fast his giant brown legs were all but a blur. In the air he could smell his sisters and brothers closing in. The glowing ferns and ivy snagged at his giant paws and his golden brown, grey flecked face. However, he took no notice. His pack needed him and that was all that mattered.

The old hound howled again and more howls came calling back. The Night Hounds surrounded their Alpha on all sides, the beasts' chests vibrating from their deep growls. They licked and chomped their sharp jaws together. They drove on, winding their way down the well-trodden path of the vibrant, radiating forest surrounding them on either side. They followed the call of those further away. The pull grew so intense the pack ran faster still.

Suddenly they came to a halt. There in front was a clearing. All was quiet. There wasn't any breeze in the Underverse to break the silence. The pack's fur stood up on end like stiff broom bristles. Something was definitely wrong. This clearing should not have even been here…

What was once luscious, colourful forest now lay lifeless. Their once-brilliant light sapped from their very core. In the middle however was one break in all the lifeless light. A patch of vibrant red.

Slowly, the Alpha's legs strode out to the bundle of red pile. Little clouds of ash billowing around his gigantic paws made his leathery nose itch uncomfortably. His legs were so long it didn't take long to reach the patch of colour. Suddenly the red moved. He heard a muffled moan. The Alpha paused, his ears flicking back and forth. For the first time in his Night Hound life he felt something. A bubbling sensation built up in the back of his mind and unable to control it any longer, nudged the bundle of red before him. Underneath it the Alpha saw another creature bundled up inside. The Alpha had not come across such a creature before. A creature with four naked, long limbs and a head covered in dark fizzy fur on the top.

He sniffed the strange creature and as he did so something sparked inside of him. His tail twitched for a moment. In the one intake of breath he saw another memory. This one was of a different realm where the skies were the brightest of blue before turning to the blackest carpet full of bright, white diamonds that shone down on a land unlike any he and his pack knew. Where in the Underverse the sea lay black and flat, in this strange land the Alpha saw it rear and crash upon golden, sandy shores. The air moved. Roaring over tumbling waves, whistling through trees till they bowed. Grass swayed making the dry strands rustle.

The Night Hound collapsed on the ground, breathing hard. It took a moment to realise for the first time in forever he could feel everything!

"Alpha!" Turning to the voice, the leader of the hounds found one of his sisters looking at him from the other side of the clearing. The others were pacing back and forth, shaking their heads, whining as though unsure of what to do. The Alpha knew his pack wanted to follow and protect their Alpha but he also understood how scared they all were of the strange clearing and of the strange creature laying before him.

The Alpha looked at the female as an individual for the first time. Taking in her unique pattern. He never knew her name and she never asked for his. They never needed to have names. Alpha was a rank, not a name. To the Night Hounds they were all brothers and sisters, a pack and that was all that mattered but now... 'NUBIS' rang through his mind. The elderly hound shook his head as an image of a strange, glowing yellow-white orb, matching the colour of the female's long, glistening coat with a bright blue background.

The female hound continued to watch him, with her startling green eyes.

"No, that is not my name..." The old hound tried to correct her, getting up stiffly off the dusty ground, but his voice faltered. Just as it reached his lips, the name fluttered away. Instead, inside he felt a hum, a song bursting to get out. A song that was bright and alive as he felt now. Tilting his head back the old Alpha howled a mournful song.

As the old Night Hound finished he saw watching on was the entire pack. For the first time they did not reply. He couldn't breathe. His chest hurt. Fear gripped the Alpha's heart for he had realised they were looking his way but not really at him. Their eyes were glazed as though they were not really there.

The Alpha realised for the first time he was alone. It was as though he had somehow awoken from a trance but his pack had not. He alone had a Soul Song raging on inside but none of his brethren replied to its call.

The Night Hound's head turned back to the creature that lay unconscious beside him on the dusty, lifeless floor. How could one creature change him so much?

After much debating, the lone hound encouraged his entire one hundred strong pack forward. Nudging them over the edge of the clearing, up to the strange creature. Even in a trancelike state, the unknown creature still unnerved them. When they sniffed, the Alpha found he was intrigued to watch them blink, their pupils dilate, awakening from their trance.

Many staggered around, unsure of what to make of their new emotions. Despite all the strangeness there was one thing that was still part of them.

Pack, Pack, Pack!

As each of those woke, the Alpha heard their Soul Song radiating inside. Growing stronger and stronger like a beating heart.

Pack, Pack, Pack! It drummed even more loudly as his newly formed pack grew in number.

Flicking his head back, the old Night Hound howled with all his soul. His Brothers and Sisters instinctively replying back, reassuring him that their pack was safe and whole once again…but there seemed to be something or someone out of place, Nubis. The golden furred hound continued to watch on, her head tilted to the side as she stood beside the strange creature still laying on the floor. The named hound's hearts rhythm beat out of sync to the rest of the Pack. A lone wolf.

OUTSIDER! The Alpha's instinct cried out deep down inside making him and the rest of his pack of Night Hounds growl and turn on the intruder.

Chapter 1

Alpha

I was pacing back and forth, my giant paws leaving their mark in the glowing earth. Little coloured sparks from the ground settled upon my fur. Looking around, I found the other hounds too had specks of lights clinging onto their fur. They faded in and out, like a heartbeat of the land. It was…a word formed in my mind. Beautiful.

My pack obediently waited for me to give the order to move on. I knew we had to follow our instinct, to move far away from the unnatural clearing. It itched inside of my mind, like it did with the other hounds making us growl and gnash our fangs. My patience was wavering.

It was me that enforced the others to stay after dragging the unconscious creature with us just fifty strides away from the unnatural, lifeless clearing. No other brethren would touch her after their awakening. I did not blame them but for the first time in my eternal life I had questions with no answers to settle the itch. Why were my pack and I in a dreamlike state? Where did this dark haired creature…the word 'girl' surfaced from my foggy memories. I tried again, where did this girl come from? Where has the light gone from around her tiny form? Who are we and how has a Lone Wolf, by the name of Nubis, found her way into my pack without me knowing?

Two of my strongest Night Hounds, twins, two males. Their long black and white fur making them impossible to tell apart from the outside. On the inside however they were entirely different. Even though none of us could remember our names, each of my Night Hound's had their own song, a Soul Song resonating deep within them. Each beating to the rhythm of my heart. The pack's Soul Song.

Alpha, Alpha, Alpha! Their souls howled to me

deep within.

Pack, pack, pack! Sang mine in return.

I knew the strange creature was a clue to our awakening and the outsider's appearance. Nubis was a clue to the girl's appearance. The two were connected somehow. I had put them under guard. The twins I knew were more than capable for the task.

In the stillness of my pack I heard a rustle of green, glowing grass and then a murmur. Pausing in my stride, my head turned. Sharp ears pointed in anticipation. The time for the questions to be answered had begun.

"She's awake." Nubis, the outsider dared speak. My body instantly responded. My cool grey eyes boring into her now burning amber ones. A deep growl rumbled from my broad, hairy chest. The twins' ears flicked back and forth, backing off slightly as they felt my power rolling over them but unnaturally the female, Nubis, did not respond. I snapped at the named female, showing her my glistening, sharp fangs but once again, she did not yield. Instead she blinked, looking down at the girl who was waking from her deep sleep. "Good." I growled, annoyed of the outsider's ignorance. I would deal with her later. The bubbling sensation was making me impatient for answers. I turned back to the waking girl still lying on the earth, light retracting from her small form till the darkness silhouetted her.

I would have chased Nubis out of my kingdom already if I did not think she was needed. So far, the female had ignored every attempt of accepting me as her Alpha or answering any of my questions. She had not looked away from the dark-haired girl since we had found her in the barren land. If I got the answers from the girl I would do just that. My chest swelled as I sat on my hunches, waiting for the girl to sit up. Yes, Nubis will yield one way or other. Bow down as me as her Alpha or be cast out. I hummed. Inside I felt... content.

I felt my pack move in closer, enclosing on the five of us. Their Alpha, the outsider, the girl and their guards - the twins. One hundred souls surrounding my beating heart while the two were still out of sync. The girl's fluttered. It wasn't as unpleasant as Nubis'. The girl's was a close match just missing the pack's by half a beat. Her Soul Song was loud and pure. An image of fluttering feathers catching a gentle breeze, a rustle of a falling leaf and a tumble of a white crested wave drifted across my inner eye. I breathed out. If it was not for her difference in appearance, the girl would naturally have a place in my pack while Nubis however, would not. For she had no song howling deep within. I closed my eyes for a brief moment as internally I shuddered. Nubis was unnatural.

I opened them again to find Nubis edging in closer to the dark haired girl, their noses nearly touching. The female hound's ears twitched back and forth. It was as though she was...concerned about the girl.

I snarled a warning. I would not allow the Night Hound with no Soul Song to touch the girl.

An uncontrollable wave of...guardianship... protectiveness overwhelmed me. The same feeling I felt towards the pack, I too felt towards the girl. Was the girl part of my pack already? My ears swivelling as I listened internally. The breath I didn't know I held escaped me. No, she was still independent yet...as part of me as much as my pack was. A strange wave of curiosity circulated my veins till they burnt like the calling to get far away from the dark land.

I saw the small eyes of the girl blink. I felt a twinge in my stomach as she looked at Nubis first but then slowly, with her mouth wide open in a strange way, turned. Taking in what must have been an awe-inspiring sight of my mighty pack till her eyes fell on my own. I felt the swell of pride envelope me for my pack was indeed mighty. Mine, my own. All our hearts beating as one.

Alpha, Alpha, Alpha! Their Soul Songs sang loudly.

Pack, pack, pack! Mine sang in return.

As I looked into the girl's eyes I saw they were brown flecked with gold around the edges. They shone, dancing with the rhythmic light around my pack and I.

I heard her heart change beat. I could smell...fear but it was like there was something else, another layer to her heart and soul. Though a tiny girl on the surface I sensed a formidable warrior lying in wait just beneath the surface. My mind swirled with too many questions...how curious this little creature was.

Chapter 2

Outsiders

"Where am I?" The girl asked. The strange line of hairs above her eyes came down. Though we Night Hounds did not have such facial expressions, her Soul Song told me all I needed to know. She was lost and very sad as though she was missing something…

"You are in the Underverse." I replied. The only answer I could give her. The young girl looked around once again. I could see her eyes widening, focusing on my pack, then her surroundings and lastly on the radiant light gravitating to me and my pack until it glowed pure white around our feet. Our fur coats glistening in its radiance and tiny sparks. Whereas the light around the girl's feet was nothing but pitch black. I felt my fur above my eyes come down. A memory slowly came into focus. The feeling was called…confusion. I listened to her Soul Song once again and realised the girl and I felt the same. United in our…curiosity.

I felt her heart grow heavy. Her Soul Song shifted, a picture came to mind of a lone wolf howling on a cold night. A white glowing orb shining in a clear diamond lit sky. I licked my fangs trying to wash away the wave of guardianship I felt once again. She was not part of my pack, so why would I feel the need to protect this girl?

"What's the Underverse?" The dark haired girl asked. Her golden framed eyes now on my hard, stone grey. I heard and felt a few members of my pack whine, shifting their feet on the hard soil. I did not blame them but in the face of an unknown creature and an outsider instinct would not allow myself to show any weakness. I continued to watch the girl, considering my reply carefully.

"We do not know." I replied in a flat tone, allowing my instinct to take over.

The girl stood up. Surrounded by my mighty pack, I was surprised to find she showed not even a glimmer of fear I felt within. She was a mighty warrior indeed.

I tilted my head, considering her for a moment. The girl was tiny in comparison to any of my hounds.

Not even a head above my fur covered elbow. Even the outsider, Nubis the smallest of all the Night Hounds was a head bigger than her. And yet…

I crouched, growling and snarling. My pack wanted to join me but I sang out to them now to hold. I was testing her. Seeing if she stood her ground. I crept closer and closer, encircling her a few times. Though I felt her small form tremble, feeling the tiny vibrations with my sensitive padded feet, the girl stayed where she was. Not out of fear but with the knowledge that if she ran, her life would be forfeited. Her eyes never left mine, facing her enemy head-on. Though my kin and I had no memory of our previous lives, our instinct ruled all, it told us to stand tall and stand our ground when challenged. It was the will of a Night Hound, the will of our nature and here she was. Nowhere near a Night Hound on the outside but on the inside…there was something behind those eyes. Our hearts beating fast, hers fluttering slightly out of sync to mine. Something that connected us both within our Soul Songs.

"What's your name?" I questioned her in a gravelly voice as I circled her slowly. My stride being so long and her frame being so small I made it around twice before she answered me.

In the corner of my eye I could see the golden-furred Night Hound, Nubis, tilt her head sideways as though intrigued with what was happening in front of her. I growled deeply, snapping at the female's feet with my teeth but the golden hound infuriated me even more by not even attempting to get out of my reach.

"Ebony Night." The girl's voice trembling slightly, for the first time she allowed her fears to bubble to the surface but again the girl did not run. I turned my gaze on hers and found she too had her head tilted. Before I could even question it, her next question court me off guard, "What's yours?" She asked. I stopped mid-stride. Blinked. Our eyes locking. As they did something happened. As the calling to run from the barren land clawed in the back of my mind so did something else, a feeling I had never felt before tonight. A dark hole threatening to envelope everything, like the darkness around the girl's feet. I searched for an answer within myself. I realised then I was afraid to answer her...Never before had I experienced such an emotion. I felt the pack shift where they sat. They felt it too, rippling through me. Inside my Night Hound's instinct snapped its jaws. No! I will focus. I will not show fear. I am…

Alpha! Alpha! Alpha! My Soul Song howled internally to me.

PACK! PACK! PACK! Their presence calmed my beating heart.

"I do not know," came my answer after a few more moments. No fear or shame echoed in my voice as I buried it deep down within.

"Why, don't you remember?" She asked. My pack moved then, unable to contain themselves any longer. Being their Alpha, I could bury my fear by instinct and will for I was the strongest in body, mind and Soul Song, but the fear was no match for the lower ranked members of my pack. They did not hear other Soul Songs as clearly as I did. Their Soul Song sang so loud in my head and heart I thought their notes would burst through my chest with its almighty power.

Alpha, Alpha, Alpha!

Pack, pack, pack!

The pack started to circle. A few braver members of my brothers and sisters broke away and stepped between me and the girl calling herself Ebony Night, but when they glanced back at me they quickly moved away to re-join the others. Their fangs flashing in the multi-coloured light. Snarling and biting the air. I saw each hair on their shoulders standing up on end. I had to act fast if I was not to allow their fear to take control.

The only ones who never left their post were the twins who closely guarded the outsider, Nubis. She did not move, so neither did they. My heart filled with pride seeing the bravery of my brothers and sisters. My chest rumbled, reverberated with commands to stand down, hold back and continue to watch on. Each one slowly but surely sat back on their haunches, doing as I asked.

I licked my teeth, pondering what to do next. For the first time the girl stepped back. I heard and felt her heart leap. Despite her bravery, she was not numb to the presence of an Alpha in front of her or the power of my pack washing over her. She may be a warrior but she clearly was not an Alpha. My tail twitched once as my chest rumbled pleasantly. I was pleased with this conclusion.

"We do not know." I decided to answer her question. Maybe she would answer honestly in return. "We are the Night Hounds, creatures of the Underverse where we have lived for a length of time we do not remember." As I told her all I knew, I watched her closely. Her bare foot moved again. Not backwards but forwards now. She moved in such silence I was surprised her feet were not padded like those of my kind. I felt again the pull of my pack wishing to run out and protect their Alpha, the black hole of fear ready to swallow them whole but I was not afraid of this little girl...not now but only what her appearance meant. "We found you in an unnatural clearing." I continued, looking up at the black sky above, nothing like the diamond studded one I saw so clearly in my mind when my pack and I were awakened from our walking sleep. My heart for a moment turned cold. The sky seemed so empty. Lifeless. I looked back at the pack, reassured they were still there. I took a deep breath, the cool air filling my enormous lungs. "No light emitted from underneath you, just as it doesn't now." I watched as the girl looked at her feet and then back at me. Her Soul Song sang of loneliness. There was that strange feeling once again.

Protect, protect, protect! The entire pack's Soul Song sang internally for their Alpha, not for the dark-haired girl like I was feeling deep within. I locked it away with a shudder.

"When we came close to you," I continued, shaking my head slightly trying to rid of the buzzing fogging my mind. "we saw things we have never seen in this world. You woke us, Ebony Night. We were alive but we were numb of all emotion. Unaware of the world around us. How do you have the powers that awaken us from our walking sleep, Ebony Night? How did you come to be here?"

The heartbeats of my pack filled my ears as they too longed for the answers ever since we had found this strange creature called Ebony Night whose heart beat just out of sync with our own.

"I do not know." She replied and all at once my pack began to howl. The sound reverberated the wooden walls of the forest around us. The only Soul

Songs that did not join in was my own and of course, the outsider, Nubis. I refused to allow the black hole of hopelessness to envelope us all despite the pull of the call.

Pack, pack, pack!

Protect! Protect! Protect!

I watched the girl throw her hands over her ears. The volume too much for her tiny ears. Her expression I could not read, but inside I felt her Soul Song stir with our own. Nubis however, her Soul

Song still did not resonate. Its silence was the loudest of them all.

Chapter 3

Pack!

I moved my pack on quickly. Far away from the unnatural clearing as we could. The two outsiders were left guarded closely by the twin brothers to follow in our wake.

I knew my hounds would soon forget their fears. Our instinct to run wild and free took over everything.

We ran south. I knew the lone Night Hound, Nubis, would not find a problem running alongside the pack but I expected the girl, Ebony Night, to fall far behind. Struggling to keep up with her tiny form running on two short legs not four padded feet but there was something even more stranger about her than I first thought. She kept up with my pack! Even when I barked an order to move faster. It was as though she never grew tired. Unlike the light around her, her energy never faded into the night.

I found a new emotion… enjoyment as I watched the pack run. The pack was strong and powerful. I was intrigued as I watched sparks from the ground, being kicked up by our four hundred padded paws, dancing across the Night Hounds' fur. I also found enjoyment in the other Underverse's delights. The low lighting casting colourful shadows around us. In those moments each of us found our fears were left far behind us. We kept on running.

Ebony Night's Soul Song seemed to have grown stronger and happier in the short time also. Her whole soul hummed with the drumming of our padded feet.

We ran all night and when the new day dawned, the land around us woke up, bursting into colourful life. Its colours shinning brighter than ever before. The dancing sparks intensified and I commanded the pack to stop to rest.

The entire pack panted, all of us breathing in and out to the same heavy rhythm. For the first time, we felt tired but alive! Hearts bumping, heat surging through our shaking, aching muscles and still the call to run sang to us from far away, enticing us closer. But I knew for now we must stop and rest.

As the others lay down, the urge to check on the two outsiders became overwhelming, making my fangs grind against one another as I made my way over. The creatures I was seeking came into sight.

The next emotion hit me like a tree falling down on top of me. I paused mid stride.

Before me the twins, who were similar on the outside in every way, told apart only by their Soul Songs, were exhausted. However, the brothers were still committed to their duty given to them by myself, their Alpha. I knew a well-earned rest and my pack would be at full strength once again but what I found made fear claw at the edges of my mind like an untameable beast.

The girl, Ebony Night who ran with such lightness she may have had padded feet, was talking to Nubis. My sharp ears had no difficulty at all to pick up Nubis' quiet, calming voice as she spoke to the young girl. But the two weren't panting, they didn't even look tired. Both the hound and the girl looked like they could have ran another day and night without even stopping…

I shook my silver flecked brown head, regathering my thoughts. I was Alpha and as such I would not show weakness in front of them or any of my pack. Be it physically or mentally. I gathered myself together. Pushing down all my newfound emotions into a ball, locking it away in the back of my mind.

Pack! Pack! Pack! My Soul Song radiated.

Alpha, Alpha, Alpha! The pack howled soulfully back. With their help, a blanket of calm wrapped itself around me. I took a deep intake of cool air, filling my lungs to their maximum. My eyes fluttered closed for a moment. My pack, my salvation.

My eyes snapped open for I felt the outsiders' eyes on me now. Silent alarm bells rang inside, her eyes made my skin crawl. My chest rumbled with a low, almost inaudible tone to those with less keen ears. The twins bowed their heads in unison as I passed. "Rest." I told them and they obeyed. Lying down, their movements mirrored one another.

I echoed my strength, power and leadership into

each stride and each pad of my gigantic clawed paws. My steel-grey eyes on the brown, golden framed eyes of the girl, Ebony Night. My Soul Song swelled inside of me. She showed me respect. Her eyes full of awe in the presence of such a powerful Alpha, then something happened I did not expect. As we continued to look at one another, something inside myself shifted. A new emotion. Recognition, deep within my heart. Questions bubbled away without my permission, the most pronounced question of all, how do I know you? Her Soul Song changed beat, matching my own in each and every way. Her reply to my question.

Pack! Pack! Pack! Ebony's and the rest of the pack sang to me in one, harmonious beat.

Pack, pack, pack! My own sang back to them all.

I stopped in front of her, my body towering over the girl's. My light now a claw length away from her naked toes. Though different in form, our Soul Songs were now unified. Opposite to the twins, on the outside she was different in each and every way but on the inside we were the same. Ebony Night was now part of my pack.

"Welcome Ebony Night." My voice a low rumble that shook the ground beneath her blackened feet where the dusty dirt clung to her. My tone and aura radiating power and authority.

The dark haired girl bowed her head so low her chin touched her chest, exposing the back of her neck where her hair fell away. A mark of respect.

Pack! Pack! Pack! My Soul Song sang.

Alpha! Alpha! Alpha! Her's sung back to me once again.

I threw my head back, howling to the black sky. In response all but one of the Night Hounds sat up and sang to their Alpha. Including one little girl who, despite everything had found her place in my pack's Soul Song and in my once cold stone heart.

Chapter 4

Memories

*T*he strange protectiveness I felt earlier was stronger than ever before.

My pack was part of me. Our hearts beat in one harmonious beat.

Alpha! Alpha! Alpha!

Pack, pack, pack!

Our Soul Song sang the same song but this one voice, this one little girl seemed to be more. It was as though she was part of me.

While my pack rested, I took it upon myself to watch over this strange little creature that stumbled into my world, waking us from our walking sleep.

I took her away from the outsider, Nubis. I would not allow such a Night Hound without a Soul Song to influence one of my own.

Unsure what she may have said during the journey, I made sure Ebony Night stayed close to me now. Commanding her to lay down on the ground not too far from my chosen spot, a bed of lush green glowing grass on top of a jagged cliff which dropped down to the still, black sea below. I was saddened to feel the girl's Soul Song tainted with sadness. Even though she was part of my pack, the nature around us did not accept her, resulting in the grass turning black and lifeless around her feet.

I blew her dark, frizzy hair gently with my hot breath. The girl looked up at me, unable to read her expression I hummed with content as I heard her Soul Song skipped with merriment. A strange noise came from her vocal cords. I too felt my throat tighten, a gravely sort of noise matching the fluidity of her higher tone…Amusement. "What a strange little thing you truly are." I said, nodding my head commandingly and without another word she lay down on the soft bed of grass a few paces away from the edge I chose, obeying her Alpha.

***

Unlike the images stirred by the girl's presence, there were no gusts to knock me over the edge.

With the girl far enough from the one calling herself Nubis, but still near enough for me to see and hear their every move, I flopped down content.

However, time ticked by and I continued to watch Ebony Night's small form. Wave after wave of new emotions washed over me. It took me some time but one by one I eventually recognised them all. Concern, protectiveness, loyalty and pride. Everything I felt towards each and every member of my Night Hounds but there was something more. Stronger, glowing in the centre of my beating chest.

It wasn't only me who was finding it hard to sleep, finding it hard to shut out the new world we had woken up in. Alive, beating with the rhythm of the pack. I understood. The pounding of the pack's heart was wild, enticing and overwhelming, if you were not used to its calling.

Even when my pack and I were in our dreamlike state, I at times found it hard not to throw my head back, howling at the black sky until the land vibrated from the powerful call. It's light dancing in time to our joint song.

The girl tossed and turned, clutching at her head uncomfortably. My Soul Song hummed until my chest reverberated in response. "Ebony Night," I called to her. "Come here please." My voice was low, quiet but gentle as though I was speaking to a pup. Again the overwhelming feeling of familiarity when I looked into her golden framed, brown eyes until my whole heart, soul and body hummed. The Underverse's light glowed to the rhythm.

Protect, protect, protect!

Obediently, the young girl came over. "Sit with me." I said and she did. There was no fear from her now. Not even the slightest shake. She had accepted me as one of her own kin and I her. She was young and when she grew, I knew she would make a fine pack member, my little warrior. I was honoured to have her by my side.

We sat together. One side of my giant hound form exposed to the nothingness beyond the Underverse' empty sea and the other, a comfortable pressure pressed against my shoulder. I felt the girl wiggle, snuggling into my warm grey flecked fur.

"Are you cold?" I asked. My voice echoing the concern I felt towards her, for the first time since…since I began to remember. It became apparent to me it wasn't weakness but strength. Strength to show such an honourable and brave creature such…love.

"A little." The girl's quiet voice replied. I lifted my

head and took in her appearance. I remember when I first saw Ebony Night she was enveloped in a bright colour of vivid magenta, her hair jet black like the ground below her feet. Now however she seemed paler, faded somehow.

My Soul Song reached out to her like a giant paw and I felt hers do the same. A strange expression broke across the girl's face. If it wasn't for the connection, I would not have known she felt happy, content and that's what she was showing me now.

I felt a flood of emotions and it took all my will not to howl against its torrent.

Unable to bear her brown golden flecked eyes on me any longer, I lifted up my long furry tail and wrapped it around her. "Sleep." I told her simply, and sleep she did. One by one the Night Hounds went off to sleep until I was the only one still wide awake. I lifted up my head. My eyes glued on the black sky above. I felt for the first time in…I don't know how long, empty. I missed the diamonds the strange little girl showed me when we first met like I knew them personally. I looked down at Ebony Night, her faded, pale form bright against the blackened ground around us. Pausing for a moment an idea came to me. I hesitated and then bending down, my black leathery nose close to her head took in a deep breath. Instantly the sky came alive. A memory, awakening in my heart. My Soul Song soared with joy as two plough shapes appeared before my eyes. I knew they meant something to me but what? I could not quite hold on to the distant memory long enough to make it make sense.

I blinked and the diamonds vanished as quickly as they appeared. My song quietened. A sense of loss and longing overwhelmed me.

I looked down at Ebony Night again, fast sleep, warm and comforted by my heart beat. I considered for a moment to take another intake of her scent but to feel the same loss again would be unbearable.

I continued to watch the pale girl. She muttered a few times in her sleep and her face scrunched up a little. Her Soul Song told me that she too was trying to remember those she could not. I started to hum. A song I felt I knew but the meaning lost long ago. I was content to see it soothe her back to sleep.

I hummed again, the words gone from me in the sands of time, too stubborn to stay put. I listened to my pack's Soul Song and together they hummed to the beat. I felt Ebony Night roll over. Her hand reached up, her ever so tiny fingers resting on my giant leathery, black nose.

"Sleep well, Raff." She said. Her words muffled against my coat but her words were full of warmth and, after a few blinks, I did.

Chapter 5

Alpha's Song

My sharp eyes snapped opened. They focused on the dark sky and a veil of a memory shimmered over it. Black dotted with silver pearls but that soon disappeared. I blinked. The lost memory leaving its scar.

I breathed out, the rush of air rolling over the dull glowing blades of grass till they swayed back and forth with its motion.

Before I lowered my stone grey eyes I knew she was still there. I could feel the girl's little fluttering heartbeat.

Pack, pack, pack! It sang.

Laid across my brown and grey flecked snout was the tiny form of Ebony Night. I felt her move, she rolled, her face now in my line of sight. I could not read her expression but the girl's Soul Song was telling me she felt content, warm and safe. I, however, still felt troubled. Her face seemed to glow but unlike the landscape around us, its pale surface reflecting the green, browns and mauves of the ground making her look ill.

I looked around her tiny form, the Underverse's light had backed away from her even further. My heart plummeted.

Just then, Ebony Night's heart sped up and her eyes fluttered open. Mouth broadened. My tail swished, once, twice, three times as I felt she was pleased to see me. Untucking her arm from beneath her head the dark haired girl placed her tiny, gentle fingers on my forehead.

"Good Night Little Fighter." I greeted her, my grey iris's warming to her touch. The tip of my long tail lay protectively upon her ghostly body, keeping her pale form as warm as possible.

Once again, her mouth widened but Ebony Night was only yawning. She stretched her tiny form, her arms waving all over the place.

I felt the familiar sensation from the night before. The word, forming in the back of my still forgotten memory. I felt my belly and lungs move. A strange noise escaping me.

Laughter.

Ebony Night smiled and I smiled in response. I felt

rather than saw all members of my mighty pack waking up and looking in our direction but for the first time I did not care what they thought of me. This little girl had awoken a part of me, an important part of me which I had lost.

I stopped, my eyes leaking with a strange wet liquid.

"What have you done to me?" I wanted to ask her but I knew it was no use for this little, dark haired girl would not know. Like the rest of us, the girl had gaps in her memory.

***

My pack and I wanted to move on. The calling to move southwards, to find a new territory grew stronger and stronger as the night wore on.

Though I could feel every single Soul Song in my heart, there was one I could not. Nubis.

Not wanting my newest member of the pack to be anywhere near the intruder, I reluctantly left the girl to run with the youngest of the Soul Songs, a small group of juveniles in my Night Hound pack, while I checked up on the brothers. Some brown, some light silver and some dark grey. The juveniles fur littered with the Underverse's sparks of light. They whined at first, not wishing to have such a strange creature in their midst - but with just one snap of my jaws they cowered and obeyed. Tails between their legs. The girl may be strange to them but she was part of our pack, part of our Soul Song, part of... me. Whether they liked it or not.

I made my way down the line of four hundred thundering paws to the twin brothers, their heads bowing low in respect, as I came over to inspect their prisoner. She, however, watched me closely. I snapped my teeth at the female Night Hound, my hackles raised high, my growl deep, my teeth gnashing but still she did not flinch. She wasn't brave, she was simply unnatural.

Nubis looked me in the eye like she was my equal. I felt infuriated. I was about to bring her to justice when I noticed her eyes shift in colour and tone. From icy grey, to golden framed brown to a burning amber. My pace faltered, allowing the brothers and their prisoner to run on. I shook my head...

"Raff?" As much as I heard the soft voice with my sharp, furry ears, I felt her small voice calling to me internally. I licked my lips and with only a few bounds I raced ahead of the brothers and their prisoner. Passed the hundreds of pounding paws, their thunder matching my ever increasing heart beat as I bounded my way to the member of my pack beckoning me.

"Ebony Night?" I called her, my gigantic body towered over my packs. They snarled. Not at me but for me, for the girl, Ebony Night. They parted, allowing me to pass more easily. My hounds slowed their pace until I was the only one running. What I saw next made my heart falter. I found the girl paler as the white light around our gigantic paws. I saw her trip and with my snout I caught her just in time. Putting her back on her feet. My entire pack encircled us. Watching, waiting, guarding.

Only a few minutes had passed since I had left her. Where once she was full of energy and life, now she was lacking in both.

"Ebony Night." My voice softening as my leathery nose nudged her face. Ice cold. It was even a struggle for her little head to look up at me with weary eyes. "Are you alright, Ebony Night?" She nodded, her determination would have outweighed any Night Hound but I could see the truth in her dying light and body. Her heart was beating more slowly than before but it was her Soul Song who was most worrying of all. It was quiet, even to my sharp furry Alpha ears. This girl was fading from this world.

"Come." I simply said, commanding her to climb up on my back. No arguments, no refusal. I was her Alpha after all. No Night Hound surrounding us would dare question their Alpha.

The girl was so small, so light I could hardly feel her where she sat.

As I wound my way through my hundred strong pack figuring out what to do, I lifted my head high. This girl, though little in size - was a part of us, a part of our pack and one day, I could feel in my heart, would make one of our fiercest fighters…but another beast clawed and bit inside of me. For the first time as my memory served I felt anxious. This one fading light had awoken so many emotions it was becoming hard to focus.

My breathing was heavy. Not out of exhaustion but out of fear. It burnt like a raging fire as it left my lungs. Unlike before, I could not extinguish it. For a moment the pack's Soul Song vanished but that was not my concern. The girl was dying and I was surprised to find I cared for her more than I cared for my pack…

"Maybe you should leave her behind?" A voice questioned me from behind.

I turned sharply, a loud, deep growl roaring from my aching chest. "Who said that?" I demanded. Followed by two black and white growling Night Hounds by her side, waiting for my command to attack her was the outsider, Nubis. She inclined her head, indicating the ghost of the girl on my back.

"Maybe you should leave her behind." She repeated. "That's what a true Alpha of such a mighty pack of Night Hounds would have done." Her eyes flashed till it settled to a stormy grey…like my own. I growled, my pack's song filling my entire soul, heart and mind. My heart thundered until it filled every Night Hound. Their bodies vibrating with the voice of their Alpha and in response they too crouched down, snarling, flashing their teeth at the unnatural beast named Nubis.

Still the strange Night Hound with no Soul Song did not shift her gaze. "Leave her behind Raff, Alpha of the Underverse's Night Hound pack. You see her light fading. Ebony Night is not of this world. Though you have claimed her as your own kind, she is not a Night Hound and soon she will leave this realm forever. You will forget everything you had known about the young girl and with her face long gone from your memory, once again you and your Night Hounds will fall into your walking sleep. Everything will go back to the way it was. I can promise you that. You and your kind will become wild and free. Without emotion and memory. Is that not what you want? Let the child die and you will live on once more without a single worry."

I felt Ebony Night fall against my back. Her heart beat impossibly slowing even more. Her Soul Song fading. As strong as I was, I could not look at her pale form. Instead I looked at my pack. Their eyes, blues, greens and browns all looked at me with sympathy. Though they did not understand, as did I, why they cared about this girl she was now part of our pack, our family, a part of a clue as to why we are here. I was not going to allow myself to let her go.

"NO!" My teeth flashed, clashing down on top of one another like a thunder clap.

Alpha! Alpha! Alpha! The pack's Soul Song chanted in response.

I turned, placing her lifeless form at the feet of the twin brother's feet. I knew they wanted to back away from the unnatural darkness which was now swallowing up the land where they stood but still the hounds did not move. She was part of me and so part of my pack. They would guard her fading form even if it meant their lives. Their loyalty was to me. To their Alpha. To our pack.

"Let the child die." The golden furred Night Hound repeated, stepping forwards until she was two strides away from me. We started to circle each other.

With the twin brothers now either side of their new charge, the girl, the other members of my pack growled as they circled around the five of us.

FIGHT, FIGHT, FIGHT!

Alpha, Alpha, Alpha! They sang loudly inside of me.

Their growls a constant vibration against my

eardrums. Their teeth flashed in the natural light of the Underverse. They licked their fangs, chomped at the air. Desperate to join their Alpha in the fight but they knew this was a fight of power, of status and unless they wanted to challenge me themselves, they had to keep their distance.

"NO!" I roared, my new emotions seemed to tear itself from my galloping heart.

Ebony Night! It beat.

I leapt forward, ready to lay my life down for hers and my pack.

"Raff, NO!" I heard the young girl's voice raise above all the Night Hounds growls and snarling, making my ears ring shrilly. I found her impossibly between me and Nubis, the outsider. My teeth about to tear into her small form. I yelped, rolling my body so I could change course. I hit the hard, black ground in front of Ebony Night's feet. The ghostly child slowly came into focus as I looked up at her. I couldn't move from where I lay on my side. My eyes widened, my pack yelped, for her light glowed icy cold. Her body looked like death itself. However, her Soul Song sang much louder than ever before.

"Please don't fight." She told me, her hand soothed my shaking body. All the Night Hounds from our pack were listening, not to her voice but to her Soul Song. So strong now it drilled into the back of our minds until something else surfaced.

Alpha, Alpha, Alpha! The girl's soul sang.

Pack, pack, pack! All the Night Hounds, including my own, howled back. My grey eyes grew wide.

Chapter 6

Transform

My body felt like it was set alight. I heard the Night Hounds cry out in pain and I too joined them in their howl. Our bodies shaking, burning internally. I felt my limbs shortening, my face changing and my fur retracting. I curled up in a ball. Praying for it to be over until, finally, sweet relief. My body relaxed, my heart slowed and I looked up. There standing over me was Nubis, the golden furred Night Hound, the outsider looking down at me but thoughts were only for the girl who lay beside her, Ebony Night. Her skin shimmering ghost like in the ever changing light.

Alpha! Alpha! Alpha! The call seemed to radiate from her shimmering, pale body. Although no longer conscious, her heart and soul continued to sing.

Pack! Pack! Pack!

Mine and the other hundred souls sang back to the young, dark-haired girl. The pack and I moved, standing up wide eyed as we took in each other's forms. Instead of giant hounds of all sorts of colours ranging from blacks, blues, greys, white and browns we were all now standing on two legs not four. Our Night Hound scratching just below the surface of our now non-furred forms which looked just like the girls.

I looked back at Nubis, the only Night Hound standing in our midst. My grey eyes watering from being unable to blink for so long. From her, golden mist rolled off her wavy, golden fur. Blowing in a breeze that was not there. The mist thickened, enveloping every soul until one by one the humans/Night Hounds vanished from my sight and their Soul Song silenced. The quietness was deafening to me.

Panic gripped my heart. "Ebony!" I cried out in alarm, reaching forward with my now naked, human fingers but I could not catch hold of her. My arms empty as her ghostly body passed right through mine. "What's happening to her?" I barked. Even in my new human form my voice still held the essence of the Night Hound I once was.

"She is not part of this world." Nubis replied simply. "She is fading and soon will be nothing but a lost memory."

I tried to take hold of her ghostly fingers with my own as her body rose up and down eerily in Nubis' golden mist but once again they passed right through her. My hound howled inside, pining for her loss in the packs Soul Song.

"Help me!" I roared at the strange Night Hound but my voice shook, reflecting my body. I felt cold. Not because of the mist, but because I was about to lose this strange little girl who found her way into my pack and Soul Song. I did not want to forget such a heartbeat that beat alongside my own.

"I cannot." Nubis told me, now walking up to what was left of the dark haired girl. Nubis may had been small when I was a Night Hound, now however she was on eye level with me. I felt a pressure. As my eyes tore themselves away from the little girl's ghostly form, which was bobbing up and down to the ebb and flow of Nubis' mist, I saw the Night Hound's ever-changing eyes were now on me. Her head tilting the way it did, making her ears flop to one side.

"Who are you?" I asked as I watched her eyes once again transform into another shade of colour. From recognisable greys, blues and then, finally Ebony's golden framed brown. I blinked.

"Now you ask the correct question." She told me sitting down on her hunches. "I am Nubis." She paused. She was testing my patience. My new human fingers opening and closing, trying to relax my tense muscles as I waited with bated breath for the answers. I felt my Night Hound clawing, fighting his way to the surface. Patience, I told him - like my Night Hound half was a separate entity.

"You gave the call." I said. It wasn't a question; it was a memory.

"Yes." Nubis answered, inclining her head once. Her eyes still focused on me. I saw her pupils change shape as she watched my expression harden.

77

"You were the voice calling us south."

"Yes." She encouraged me.

"Then you are not a Night Hound?"

"Not quite." She corrected me, standing up and walking around the once dark haired girl. My heart thumped louder. Her Soul Song would soon be on its final verse; I could feel it. Nubis sat beside me. My heart hammering against my newly formed rib cage. This new chest did not seem large enough to contain it.

I felt the strange pressure once again. Nubis was watching me and I gave my full attention. Whoever and whatever she was I knew she had the answers of how to help the girl whom my heart and soul sang for.

PROTECT, PROTECT, PROTECT. It cried so loud.

"I am Nubis. I am the messenger of The Star Dog and guardian of the gates between worlds, Canis Major."

In front of my eyes were a flash. I stumbled back. It wasn't so much the pain I felt, but a memory forming in the back of my mind that made me falter. "I am sorry," Nubis, messenger of Canis Major continued to look at me. Her eyes full of...pity? "Memories hurt but you must choose to remember if you choose to save this girl."

"I do." The words left my newly formed lips quicker than I could think of them.

"Then remember your former life, you must." Said the hound with golden mist rolling off her golden waving fur. "You have been here far too long Raff, Alpha of the Night Hounds. You and your pack have lost the memories of who you truly are." My eyes grew wide. What did she just say? Words failing me this time. Nubis nodded as though she understood my silent question ringing through my mind. "I set you free." She announced to me. Her fur began to ripple even more. I watched in amazement as it seemed to stretch and then, retract! The female hound stood up onto her hind quarters. Her forelimbs shrank while her hind quarters elongated very slightly. Underneath the retracting fur bare humanoid skin, tickled by her own golden mist still swirling around us.

The mist seemed to cling to her, solidifying, covering her with golden robes. Her golden, glittering hair now flowed from the top of Nubis' head and down her back. Mist swirled around her hand as she flicked her fingers out at me, directing an impossible hurricane my way. I tried to fight my way to Ebony Night, tried taking hold of her body but, too late. I was thrown back, through the mist, over the cliff's edge waiting beyond, and then found myself falling to the impossible crashing black waves below.

Darkness, cold. All my senses I thought were alive earlier were now even more so. Set alight, coursing through me before sleeping once again as everything grew black around me.

The only thought keeping me sane as it rang through my body, heart and mind - a song in a unified drum beat kept me fighting the fire. It sang: EBONY NIGHT, EBONY NIGHT, EBONY NIGHT!

Chapter 7

Night

I was running. My humanoid feet now covered in some kind of hide. They thundered along the dry, stony ground. If I was in control of my body I would have stopped, "This was not the Underverse..." I told myself. I was being pulled along like a puppet.

My feet ached from the pounding but still I didn't stop. I felt my mouth open, cold air filling my lungs. "Come on, Stella!" I called. If I was in control I would have stumbled because as I turned, I saw a girl looking so similar to Ebony Night...but she wasn't her. It couldn't have been. Her hair was amber brown instead of the little girl's rich black.

"James, wait!" The other girl cried. Her hands desperately reaching out for mine. My soul reacting differently to that of the physical.

James...A distant rumble of memory resurfacing.

"Race ya!" I called, laughing happily but the girl called Stella was not. Her eyes were shiny, water leaked from its corners. I longed to go back to her but my body was not listening as my hands gripped hold of a rock face. Inside I gasped with awe. Above was a high tor. The sun directly above making it impossible to see the top against the blinding light.

Sun!

With my sight blinded by the pure white light, I felt my true self stumble backwards as my body continued forwards.

"James, wait for me, stop!" I heard the young girl's voice, whose were so similar to Ebony's, cry out.

As I blinked, my eyes adjusted. There in front of me was the girl, Stella. Stella's golden-framed brown eyes glittering in the torch light she now held. Looking around, I realised I was no longer standing at the bottom of the tor but somewhere completely different.

A song rose up out of the girl's raw, chewed lips. I stepped closer to her now. Nothing but a ghost to her, invisible, unable to touch. The song she sang was the same song I sang to Ebony to sooth her to sleep. The words now clear in my mind as both our bodies and souls sang the well-known, unbearable verses of love, loss and longing returned.

A few times I thought Stella could see me, her eyes shifting my way but how could she? Nubis told me I must remember…Was this a memory, a scene from long ago? I was not sure. My world had changed so much since Ebony's arrival.

I watched the girl with the brown golden framed eyes walk with her torch, still singing our song down to the many villagers waiting in the valley below. Their light and voices in the night calling to hers.

Wood Town.

My heart knew this town so well.

The first people to join her were an older man and woman of similar ages. The man was holding the lady's torch for her as he held her tightly in his arms. Stella did not look their way, her eyes were only for me now as my feet slid ghost-like over the uneven, cobbled road. The road wound its way through the top half of the village sat in the belly of the valley, to the lower half which hugged the rugged cliffs, to end eventually at the sandy shores. The older woman's voice wavered slightly, the pitch going up as her throat tightened but with a gentle squeeze on her shoulder, the man helped her continue with the verse.

With our eyes still connected, Stella's brown eyes bored into my cold grey. Why did you leave me? She seemed to ask all the while. Why did you leave?

I frowned. The expression felt strange on my newly formed face. If I had the choice, I would have never left her side. Our hearts and souls sang the same beat as my pack and Ebony Night's. This young girl was part of that pack. She was family.

Night...

We were on a beach now, sand dunes behind us and the seemingly endless sea stretching way out in front. Only a small island seemed to interrupt the horizon. There was something in the swell - a boat? Inside the small boat was a pile of belongings. As I came closer I saw books, clothing, maps, bits and pieces of scrap paper scribbled with drawings and writings of the adventures that were planned to be just around the corner.

These all belonged to me!

My mouth copied that of Ebony's when she was amazed, frightened and surprised.

I stared back as things started to click into place.

Suddenly the flames on villagers' torches seemed to burn brighter, their white light burning the back of my eyes. The truth came crashing down on me as I watched Stella's white flames streak across the blackened sky. Others joined it until both the small boat and its belongings were set alight in the Wood Town's traditional funeral ceremony. Only one voice carried above the roar of both fire and singing voices. "Goodbye James Night." I heard Stella speak softly. Her voice, gentle compared to the crashing waves and roaring fire. "I love you for all eternity. Wherever you may be."

"I Love you too, sis," my ghost replied. A tear fell, leaving an impossible mark on the sand before the scene faded away into the darkness of the night.

***

"Well done James Night." Nubis' voice drifted in amongst the brightly lit, golden mist that surrounded me once again. Her Night Hounds' body forming as the mist solidified, swirling in and out of her luscious golden fur. Her eyes currently reflecting Stella's and Ebony's.

"Where is my niece?" I growled, my Night Hound scratching just beneath the surface. But whatever powers Nubis had, she kept my Night Hound tightly locked away.

"Calm, dear one. Your pack is safe. The Night Hounds are currently asleep, dreaming of a better life on the surface. Ebony Night, on the other hand, is in fate's hands. Even the starry gods and goddesses cannot intervene with this path she must tread, but we cannot foretell if she will live or simply fade away." I growled at the threat. "However," Nubis' eyes flashed with a warning and reluctantly I contained myself. Even in human form my Night Hounds' habits could not be forgotten. "We feel you have a part to play if this girl is to proceed on the path fate has chosen for her. Be warned James Night, you cannot decide for her. Only she alone can choose to remember who she really is. For you and your pack to choose freedom from the Underverse, this girl known as Ebony Night must fight to find herself but you must help her to proceed to see the truth or she will simply fade away." Nubis' eyes grew sullen now. It was clear she knew how I felt as my Night Hound howled for my nieces' and my packs' safe return. "My father, Canis Major, gave you all a unique gift. After seeing the bravery of the once-human who is now known as Stella Maris, he grew fond of mankind." Nubis smiled kindly at me. My human form gave away my emotions too easily. "You and your kin were given your Night Hound forms so your souls would stay intact in the Underverse until the time came that he could release you."

"Ebony Night had proved herself to the mighty Star Dog when she rescued a Comet Cat from the fate no other could have comprehend. She was, however, thrust into this realm in an unforgivable manner but not even the stars themselves can intervene. This ill fate had to happen in order for this young girl to tread the path to become the person she is destined to be."

"Canis Major sent me, for I am not a god so I can wander the Underverse without tilting the balance. Yes, I was the one that howled. Yes, I was the one who sent you on your path to Ebony Night."

I grew numb. Unable to move or talk.

"My father treads the voids between the realms and can foresee futures. Not all of them certain but he knew the dark-haired girl holds the key to releasing your packs' souls to the other realm if given the means.

"Go James Night, Raff of the Night Hounds and protector of Ebony Night. The young, powerful girl who holds Ia's fate in the palm of her hands. May the starry gods and goddesses look down fondly upon you all." With that the golden Night Hound vanished from sight.

I breathed in heavily. Absorbing all the information I had learned.

"I was James Night, Ebony Night's Uncle, brother of Stella Maris, her mother." I spoke aloud, trying to make sense of everything. "I was once human. I died. My soul was transported to the Underverse. I and the other souls like mine were transformed into Night Hounds by Canis Major, the dog god from the starry sky so my soul and those of my pack could be safely returned one day to Ia."

I felt something tickle my wrist gently. Looking down I saw the golden mist twirling itself around me. A memory came back to me. The mist reminded me of a snake I once saw hiding in some long grass by my old home as a child.

"I have to find my niece, Ebony Night." I continued to tell myself. I now felt the mists' tendrils wrap itself around my legs. My heart beat fast as I watched the snakes sliver higher and higher up my body but somehow I found myself standing stock still. Was I too scared to move? "I have to help find a way back home so she can return also and fulfil her destiny…" I knew nothing of this destiny Nubis spoke about but it seems a lot for a young girl. Saying all this aloud I found helped me concentrate on the here and now. My mind was too crowded to think clearly. A million and one emotions I had not experienced for a time I cannot recall, coursed through my now human body. But even so, a few of them stood out from all the others. A beacon in the night. Loyalty, love and determination. Hope.

It was only now I realised I was not afraid. I was accepting the role I needed to play in all of this in order to return home. To return to my family once more.

"One thing for sure," I said to the mist hoping Nubis or any of the other gods and goddesses could hear me. "I'd left Stella behind all those years ago. I will not leave anyone else behind now, I will not abandon Ebony Night. Not now, not ever…Help me." I pleaded with all my heart. I watched the mist tendrils rise from where they rested on my arms and legs. They rose higher and higher until they towered high above me. The snake heads nodded, slowly, as though they were bowing their head respectfully. I watched wide-eyed for a moment before closing my eyes as they arched their back threateningly. Still I did not move for I knew I needed to face whatever challenge came my way. Even death. I took a deep breath.

"I will find you, Ebony Night." I promised and crossed my heart.

To be continued…

Other Books by A. C. Winfield

Ebony's Legacy:

* Book 1: The Star Pirate
* Book 2: The Comet Cat
* Book 3: The Night Hound
Book 4: The Fire Bear (Coming Soon)

*The Moon Owl

Galactic Saga:

Book 1: Galactic Riders
Book 2: Coming Soon

Tale of the Four Crowns:

Book 1: Quilbert and the Winter King

www.acwinfield.co.uk
Follow @acwinfield on Twitter, Facebook
& Instagram.

Quilbert and the Winter King

A.C.Winfield

Quilbert the hedgehog was a very curious hedgehog. He, his brother Thorn and his sister Hedgy asked their father about the big sleep during Winter's reign. The little hoglets were warned to stay inside their cosy burrow as winter arrived. But as the air grew chilly and the snowflakes fell from the sky, the wonders of Winter were too good for little Quilbert to stay inside.

Outside waits the Winter King...

A.C.Winfield

Galactic Riders

Book 1 of The Galactic Saga

Andrew loved everything about space. From the planets, black holes, super novas, red dwarfs and...well you get the idea. He loved it all!

What Andrew didn't imagine was that he would be on an adventure through space not only on the back of a rainbow coloured dragon, Awa, but also with his older sister, Lou.

What starts off as a dream of gliding along Eridanus, the river of solar winds, turns into a

nightmare as they discover the truth about what happens when you get chosen to be the new Galactic Riders...

The Moon Owl
A Companion to Ebony's Legacy

A.C. Winfield

As the stars come out to play Ebony begins to tell Hale, the Comet cat, and her Grandfather a bedtime story. She tells the tale of Noctua the Star Owl who hears and sees all, she is the eyes and ears of Ursa Major, the mother of all stars. Longing for a family Noctua flies down to Ia to lay her eggs but all is not well. Food is getting harder to find and the greedy Ghost Owl, Umra, is lurking in the shadows...

About the Author

A.C Winfield (Amy) grew up in St Ives (Porthia) on the west coast of Cornwall, England for 21 years before moving to her dream location, North Devon. North Devon is where Amy's heart always lived and where most of her influences come from.

School was a struggle. After being diagnosed with slight Dyslexia, Amy chose not to let it stop her from pursuing her hobbies and goals. Despite it making her exams a struggle she managed to get the GCSE's needed to get into college to study a BTEC in photography.

During college Amy started illustrating other people's characters which led to Amy putting her own characters and scenes wandering around her head onto paper.

Amy started selling her work at local fairs and events, and who were her customers? Mainly children and the utterly amazing, quirky people who seem to have a knack for being able to jump into Amy's imaginative and sometimes goofy mind.

-Ben Lincoln

Made in the USA
Columbia, SC
19 January 2018